The Lily Pad Ball

illustrated by Maggie Kneen ❦ written by Judy West

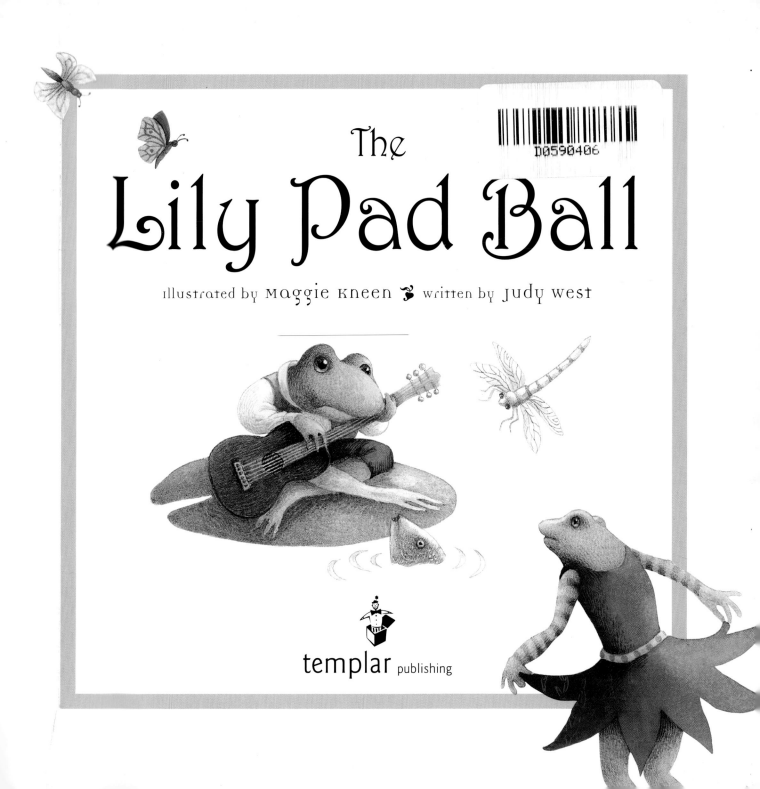

templar publishing

"We're the musicians for the woodland ball," said Ferdinand the frog, "so our music must be perfect. One more time please." All the frogs began to play, except Arabella. "Arabella, please!"

"But I want to dance," replied Arabella. "My dear," laughed Ferdinand, "frogs DON'T dance!"

"I want to dance to the music, not
play it," moaned Arabella to her mother.
"But Arabella, you're a frog," replied
her mother, "and frogs don't dance, they hop.
Now hop off to Uncle Hamish's house and see
if he's ready for the ball."

On her way she saw Monty and
Millie Mouse putting on their fine clothes.
"Look at us, little Arabella," said Monty,
"we're going to dance the night away!"
"What a fine pair we'll make," said Millie.
"I shall dance too," said Arabella.
Millie and Monty laughed.
"Not you, dear Arabella – you're a frog.
Frogs don't dance!"
Arabella frowned and hurried on.

Arabella set off
across the foxglove field.
"Hop, don't dance!" called
her mother as she went.

In the forest glade, Squirrel and Badger
were hanging lanterns and putting up flags.
"This will look fine for the dancers," said Badger.
"I'm a dancer, Mr Badger,"
said Arabella shyly.
"You!" scoffed Badger.
"You're a frog –
frogs don't dance!"

When Arabella arrived at Uncle Hamish's house,
she found him playing his bagpipes.
"Uncle Hamish, everyone says
frogs don't dance.
But I do. Can I show you?"
"Don't be silly, Arabella. Anyway,
there wouldn't be room for you

with all the mice and rabbits.
It will be quite a squash.
Now go and see if the
toads are ready, dear."

Big Cyril and the toads
were playing their drums,
practising for the finale of
the woodland ball.
"Cyril," said Arabella, over the noise,
"I want a chance to dance."

Arabella hurried home.
"Big Cyril says it's going to rain,"
she told her mother.
"The dance floor will get wet and the
mice will get their costumes soaked."
"Let's hope it stays dry," said her mother.
"Now, get into your feather dress."
But just as Arabella was setting off,
DOWN CAME THE RAIN.

"There won't be a chance for ANYBODY to dance soon," said Cyril, looking up at the sky. "It's going to rain."

It was a mighty downpour.
Water gushed down the woodland paths
and everybody arriving at the ball had to take cover.
By the time it was over, the dance floor was flooded.
"Where, oh where can we have our
woodland ball now?" wailed Uncle Hamish.

One of the littlest frogs
piped up. "Maybe we
should move the feast to
the river bank," he suggested.

"Then we could play and dance on –"

"– the LILY PADS!"

everyone chorused.

So everyone made their way
down to the river, where they
began to set things up.

The clouds moved on, the frogs' music filled
the evening air, and the ball and feast finally began.
Most animals didn't want to dance on the lily pads in
case they fell in the water. Except for one.
Everyone turned to look at...

...ARABELLA, dancing beautifully for all to see! "My goodness, frogs DO dance!" cried Arabella's mother, and everyone laughed and clapped.

For Maisie – love Maggie
For my husband and children – J.W.

A TEMPLAR BOOK

First published in the UK in 2005 by Templar Publishing,
an imprint of The Templar Company plc,
The Granary, North Street,
Dorking, Surrey, RH4 1DN, UK
www.templarco.co.uk

Illustration copyright © 2005 by Maggie Kneen
Text and design copyright © 2005
by The Templar Company plc

3 5 7 9 10 8 6 4 2

ISBN 978-1-84011-807-0

Designed by Janie Louise Hunt
Edited by Stella Gurney

Printed in Malaysia